Castaways!

adapted by Alison Inches

based on a script written by Leslie Valdes

illustrated by Warner McGee

Ready-to-Read

Simon Spotlight/Nick Jr.

New York   London   Toronto   Sydney

Based on the TV series *Nick Jr. The Backyardigans*™ as seen on Nick Jr.®

SIMON SPOTLIGHT
An imprint of Simon & Schuster Children's Publishing Division
1230 Avenue of the Americas, New York, New York 10020

Manufactured in the United States of America

4 6 8 10 9 7 5

Library of Congress Cataloging-in-Publication Data

Inches, Alison.
Castaways! / adapted by Alison Inches.—1st ed.
p. cm.—(Ready-to-read)
"Based on the TV series Nick Jr. The Backyardigans as seen on Nick Jr."
ISBN-13: 978-1-4169-0802-9
ISBN-10: 1-4169-0802-1 (pbk.)
I. Backyardigans (Television program) II. Title. III. Series.

PZ7.I355Cas 2006
[Fic]—dc22
2005012111

"Ahoy, there!" says .
UNIQUA

"Ahoy! We are castaways!"

say  and .
PABLO   TYRONE

"Our  was lost at

SHIP

sea!" says 🐧.

PABLO

"Our 🛟 had a leak!"

LIFEBOAT

🦫 adds.

TYRONE

"Now we are stuck on an ," says .
ISLAND   PABLO

"We are the only ones here," says .
TYRONE

"I am a castaway too,"

says .

AUSTIN

"I feel very shy today."

"I feel too shy
to say 'ahoy' to ,

UNIQUA

, and ."

PABLO   TYRONE

"We need to build a
HUT
in case it ☔ !"
RAINS
says .
PABLO
"I will look for ✎
WOOD
for the walls."

"Wow," says  .
PABLO

"Where did all of this

🪵 come from?
WOOD

Ahoy! Is somebody there?"

"I will look for ,"
VINES

to tie the ,"
WOOD

says .
TYRONE

Snip! Snip!

"Hey," calls TYRONE .

"Who cut these VINES ?

Ahoy! Is somebody there?"

"I will look for  LEAVES for the roof," says UNIQUA.
Swish! Swoosh!

 fall to the ground.
LEAVES

"Ahoy! Is somebody up in

the ?" asks .
TREE   UNIQUA

The castaways bring the

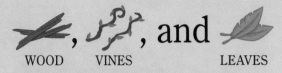, , and 🍃

WOOD   VINES   LEAVES

back to the 🐚.

BEACH

They build their .

HUT

"Wow! We built a nice

  ," says .

BEACH　　HUT　　　　　　　　UNIQUA

"Now all we need is food to eat," says  .

TYRONE

"Maybe we can catch a 🐟 ," says 🦗 .

FISH   UNIQUA

"We can build a ,"
FISHING POLE

says .
PABLO

"We have a 🪵
STICK

and a 📎 for the hook.
PAPER CLIP

All we need is some 🧶."
STRING

"Hey, where did that 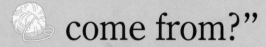 come from?"

STRING

asks .

TYRONE

"Ahoy! We are really not alone!" says .

UNIQUA

"Follow that  !"
STRING

cries .
PABLO

"Ahoy! Who can it be?"

"It is  !" says  .

AUSTIN   UNIQUA

"  did all of

AUSTIN

those things!"

" , you should have said
'Ahoy!'" tells him.

AUSTIN

UNIQUA

"I was feeling too shy

to say 'Ahoy!'" says .

AUSTIN

"But I wanted to help."

"That was very nice!"

says .

PABLO

"You are a great castaway."

"Does anyone want a snack?" asks  .

UNIQUA

"Come on! We can have island  !"

FRUIT

Ahoy!